I0634411

Nikolai

V.
Pokrovski

i

The Gospel in the Monuments of Iconography

mostly Byzantine and Russian

Nikolai

V.
Pokrovski

i

The Gospel in the Monuments of Iconography
mostly Byzantine and Russian

ISBN/EAN: 9783337295097

Printed in Europe, USA, Canada, Australia, Japan

Cover: Foto ©Andreas Hilbeck / pixelio.de

More available books at **www.hansebooks.com**

N. V. Pokrovskiĭ

T·H E

G O S P E L

IN THE MONUMENTS OF ICONOGRAPHY

mostly
BYZANTINE AND RUSSIAN

By N. Pokrovsky

With 226 pictures in the text and 12 tables.

PICTURE

ST. PETERSBURG

Appanage Press. 40 Mokhovaia St.

1892

Printed by order of the Imperial Moscow
Archaeological Society in accordance with
§56 of its statutes.

Chairman Countess Uvarov.

DEDICATED

TO THE MEMORY

OF COUNT ALEKSEY SERGEIEVICH UVAROV

THE FOUNDER OF THE IMPERIAL MOSCOW
ARCHAEOLOGICAL SOCIETY AND ORIGINATOR
OF ARCHAEOLOGICAL CONGRESSES IN RUSSIA

From the editors.

In publishing the first volume of papers of
the VIIIth Archaeological Congress, which took place
in Moscow in January, 1890, to commemorate the
twenty-fifth anniversary of the foundation of the
Imperial Miscow Archaeological Society, the editors
decided to devote it to the extensive works of the
Professor of the St.Petersburg Theological Academy,
N. V. Pokrovsky, of the Department of Ecclesiastical
Antiquities, in view of the importance of the works
and also of the necessity, in the opinion of the
editors, of bringing forth and encouraging works
dealing with the study of Byzantine-Russian Iconography
and Russian ecclesiastical antiquities in general.
All those papers of the Congress which will be de-
livered to the Moscow Archaeological Society will find
place in the succeeding volumes. The second volume,
which is devoted to prehistoric antiquities, is already in print.

This first volume was printed in St.Petersburg
under the personal supervision of the author: all the
following volumes will be printed in Moscow under the
auspices of the Moscow Archaeological Society.

Countess Uvarov.

Monuments of Gospel iconography represent one
of the greatest items in the general system of ecclesiastical archaeology: that is why we have long paid
attention to them. Little by little we have classified
them into a special group and studied them by means of
scientific publications and existing literature from
the external and inner points of view. The results did
not fulfill our original expectations. It was found
that the existing publications of Byzantine and Russian
monuments are insufficient and unreliable in the extreme. Many of the most important monuments were not
only not studied, but even not published. The choice
of monuments for publication is often explained by chance
and ulterior motives, but not by the requirements of
the essence of the matter: the pictures of the monuments
sometimes give wrong impressions of the originals, clearly contradicting the fundamental principles of Orthodox
iconography: and the existing scientific literature
merely brushes some separate questions of Gospel iconography, not touching the great mass of them, and almost
entirely ignoring the existence of the religious ideas in

the Russian monuments. In view of this, we undertook
several journeys to study the monuments in the places
of their origin - in Russia, Greece, Turkey and Western
Europe. Here there presented itself the possibility
of learning many monuments entirely unknown in scientific
literature, and of correcting inaccuracies in existing
publications and appraisals of monuments. On the basis
of this material, collected mainly through the personal
study of original monuments, the present book was con-
ceived. A relative incompleteness of material and defects
in the methods of research are unavoidable in the first
experiments with such works: but we allow ourself to
hope that in this work nothing of substantial importance
is missing and that everything has received an explanation to the author's best ability. Only those monuments
were purposely left out which, being copies of the originals, are not of great importance in the general history
of Gospel iconography. Future discoveries of monuments
might influence one way or another, some of our conclusions: but the material collected by us will hardly lose
its special significance. Our constant and warm desire
has been to publish in pictures as great as possible a
part of the collected material, since pictures present
to the reader the exact and clear conception of the subject, and give clarity to the conclusions based on them.

But the lack of necessary means forces us to restrict
the number of illustrations. We give here only pictures
of the most characteristic monuments, some hitherto un-
published and essentially necessary for a clear understanding of our descriptions and conclusions. We have
annotated by means of footnotes all the most important
publications, with the idea of facilitating for the
reader the possibility of inquiries and verifications.
If our work arouses in the readers a certain esteem
and love for Orthodox antiquity, we can with calm conscience, consider our aim attained.

St. Petersburg.   N. POKROVSKY
October, 1891

INTRODUCTION

The purpose of the present work consists in the
ecclesiastico-archaeological explanation of pictures
referring to Gospel history, mainly Byzantine and
Russian. Iconography of the Gospel in all its variety
of monuments ancient and modern, oriental and western,
artistic and craftsman, is necessarily connected with
the Gospel texts; but not always and not everywhere
does it present it with the same exactitude and uniformity. Appearing in the most ancient epoch of Christianity in simple forms, iconography with time changes
its original character, according to the change in the
attitude of Christian consciousness to the Gospel
text itself, and the general point of view on the aims
of Christian art and iconography. Therefore iconography is, up to a certain point, subordinated to the
law of historical development. Where lies the original
kernel of Gospel iconography, where and when and under
what circumstances was it developed, in what did this
development express itself, and to what end did it
arrive? These questions have their incontestable importance. The iconography of the ancient period does
not represent either a wide choice of subject or breadth

of theological and artistic planning in development of
these subjects or iconographical compositions. Everything here is simple, as simple as is the original
Christianity. The Christian symbolism of the catacombs
expresses even the most lofty truths of Christianity
in concise forms; in simple, sometimes even naive form,
it gives only a hint of these truths, leaving it to the
observer to transport himself by thought and imagination
into the region of eternal ideals which transcend the
medium of the pictorial art. Here historical scenes also
do not vary: we meet the same themes in Italy, in Greece,
in Syria, and in Egypt. The centre of this iconography
presents the personality of the Savior and the miracles
of the Gospel. But in this period neither the types
nor the composition of the pictures were yet settled
with sufficient clarity, through the trends toward this
stabilization were already noticeable in the Fourth Century. Christian art was under the strong influence of
antique art, which at that time, it is true, had lost
the freshness of energy necessary for new creation, but
preserved the beauty and plasticity of artistic forms.
Using these forms and uniting them with Christian ideals,
Christian artists, if at the same time they succeeded
in mastering the full conception of Christianity as a

religion, could not but see the extreme inadequacy of
these forms for the expression of Christian ideas. It
was necessary to remove some of these forms, as not
corresponding to the spirit of Christianity, and to change
others and create anew a third under the immediate guidance of Christianity itself. Traces of free treatment
of the original forms are already noticeable clearly in
the sculpture of ancient Christian sarcophagi; they appear even more clearly in the mosaics of the IV - V centuries, and the VI century already gives us many monuments of entirely independent Christian art, created
inside the Christian world, while antique art here left
only a trace, as a tradition of a remote artistic school.
Lively creative activity in the sphere of pure Christian
art is concentrated in Byzantium. Byzantine art delivers
a decisive blow to the plasticity of the forms of antique
art, but it considerably widens the artistic horizon and
elevates thought and imagination into the region of lofty
ideals. An immense work was ahead for Byzantium: it was
necessary to establish the fundamental types of design of
different persons, and this already demanded great historical, theological and artistic knowledge,/because
these types were not just a simple copy of nature, but

were a result of a creating, even if such creating

was not attempting to rupture the bond with realistic

portrayal: it was necessary to create entire groups

and compositions of pictures on the subjects offered

by Christianity. The work was going on rapidly and as

early as the VI century vast cycles of pictures were com-

pleted in the spirit of the Byzantine artistic stand-

point. The type of the Savior and the compositions on

Gospel themes were the subjects on which the creative

activities of the Byzantine artists had to focus them-

selves first of all. Already in the VI century there

appeared illuminated Gospels with vast iconographical

content with types and compositions sufficiently de-

fined. Whereas antiquo-Christian art sets forth mainly

concrete facts, the Byzantine art introduces into icon-

ography elements of abstract theology, profound thought

and contemplation. The main determining basis in this

activity of Byzantines and also of artists of the antiquo-

Christian period served the text of the Gospel: but

this was not the only source of knowledge of the person-

ality of Jesus Christ and Gospel history. Christian

tradition in its various aspects and forms had to find

access to iconography: in accordance with the development

of the tradition and its transition into the consciousness

of artists, iconography was also changed: new composi-

tions on the subjects of Gospel history were created,

old compositions were changed, absorbing new elements,

which appeared under the influence of the tradition.

Tracing in this way the development of iconography, we

trace simultaneously the development of religious and
                                    the
artistic conceptions: observing/gradual growth of Gos-

pel iconography we observe the change in the relation-

ship of human consciousness toward the Gospel text in

different epochs of history, and we study the efforts of

human thought to soar to the heights of the Gospel, and

to express the whole depth and breadth of its content in

artistic forms. The development of these forms con-

tinues from the V up to the XII century, but even the

ensuing period of decadence, just as in the period of
                                        the
the second renaissance of Greek history in/XVI to the

XVII centuries, presents not a few curious phenomena

in Gospel iconography, even if these phenomena were not

as much the result of organic development as a conse-

quence of mechanical combination and piling up of ele-

ments. The basic rules of Byzantine iconography were

also absorbed by the medieval art of Western Europe,

and formed the foundation of the multitude of monuments

of murals, miniatures, carvings, and enamels, pres-

Cathedral of St. Sophia in Kiev. The majority of ancient
Russian churches were satisfied in their murals by the
more comprehensible and customary pictures. Of illuminated manuscripts there could not have been many, and
in homes, simple icons were used. Also in the beginning
the total of available educational means could not have
been very great, and if in the whole complex of ancient
Russian iconography one can find in the most ancient
epoch some revelation of Russian creation, then we do
not find them in Gospel iconography.   Comparing, from
this point of view, Russian and Byzantine monuments, we
come to a conclusion of identity of forms, points of
view and conceptions appearing in them. The only conclusion to be drawn from this is the conviction that
Russian iconography is genetically dependent from the
Byzantine. But with the approach of the XVII century
the situation changes. Both the monuments that have
reached us and the clear testimony of ancient literature
assure us that our Gospel iconography begins to enrich
itself by the afflux of forms, which have their origin
partly in the neo-Greek and partly in Western icono-
graphies, and partly were created by Russian artists;
at the same time, some ancient Byzantine forms disappear
from artistic usage, or enter new combinations. This

change is again connected with the change in religious

and artistic points of view: it has reflected the

transition from the epoch of "faith from simplicity of

heart" to the epoch of knowledge by inquiry. All these

steps in the history of Byzantine and Russian art

must be given an exact explanation in the analysis of

monuments of Gospel iconography. But the mentioning of

the epochs considered shows only the general trend of

Byzantine-Russian iconography, whereas in the history

of many separate pictures one often has to deal also

with particular reasons underlying the changes and de-

velopment of some single picture, which considerably com-

plicates the task of research. It is clear from the

above that our research is directed toward archeological

and historical aims but not toward practical ones. Of

course the classification of iconographical forms and

their assignment according to epochs with the identifica-

tion of characteristics of one or another epoch can serve

as criticism in the matter of the defining of newly

founded monuments and chronological placing of them,

which already constitutes a practical result. And

one also can hardly contest the fact that correct planning
of tasks for our modern shattered iconography is possible
only through study of the monuments of antiquity, as
these monuments present many attempts to solve identical
problems at different times: the study of the experiments
of the past is useful in making plans for the future.
But at this time we leave aside the problems of practical application of archeological knowledge, as a subject of the special ecclesiastico-practical science in
conjunction with artistic technique and stay within the
limits of historico-archaeological science: scribitur
ad narrandum, non ad probandum. In what way is it possible to reach the satisfactory solution of the problems with which one confronts oneself? According to our
conviction the only possible way consists in the com-
parative study of the physical monuments of antiquity
and the monuments of ancient literature. Bringing to
light and necessary criticism of the former will show
the historical growth of the iconographical forms and
their changes in different times, and the monuments
of literature will give the explanation of the inward
basis and motives stimulating these changes. We shall
explain this.

The lack of preliminary collections and works
in the field of the history of the Gospel iconography
in Byzantium and Russia puts an investigator first of
all in the position of a collector of material. It is
impossible to set broad aims of research in the field of
archaeology until the moment when the separate monuments
are brought to light. The more we have of such monuments
the better and the nearer to the truth will be the conclusion based on them. A truthful saying was uttered a
long time ago: "He who has seen only one monument has
seen nothing and he who has seen a hundred monuments has
seen only one". It is necessary to compare these monuments and distinguish in them traces sometimes seeming-
ly petty, but which have their importance in founding
the general theses; it is necessary to classify them
according to the similarity of basic features, allocate
them according to chronological and sometimes to local
groups. This is the preliminary and preparatory stage
of the work. It is impossible to avoid it; in the same
way it is impossible to keep this material for oneself,
and not to exhibit it: because the basis on which a conclusion is reached should be set forth, otherwise veri-
fication of the conclusions is impossible. Until now
the monuments of the ancient Christian period enjoy

comparatively great repute; the Byzantine monuments are
less known, though they have already attracted the attention of the specialists, and some groups of them, such
as, for example miniatures have received even scientific-
artistic appraisal. But for the history of Byzantine
iconography, collection of the exact reproductions of the
monuments would be necessary which until now we have not
had. The attempts of this kind made by Agincourt,
Sommerar, Lacroix, Rogot de Fleury, and the others, give
only a few examples of Byzantine iconography, chosen
according to the personal judgment of the authors mentioned, not in the interest of Byzantine history as a
whole, are for us extremely insufficient. As regards
monuments of Russian iconography, they are even less
known archaeological literature than the Byzantine monuments. This creates the necessity for preliminary search
and study of the monuments dispersed in the museums of
Europe, in monasteries, cathedrals, churches and private
collections of the amateurs of antiquity. Up to what degree we were able to prevail, this first obstacle will
be seen in the proper place. Undoubtedly the attempt
made by us to write a complete history of Gospel iconography would be impossible without this preliminary work.

The possibility of the scientific coordination of monuments collected in this manner has its support in the
fundamental elements of Byzantine-Russian iconography
and does not contradict the development inherent in the
latter. The opinion that this iconography represents a
conglomerate of chance phenomena, appearing according to
the whims and caprices of the craftsman icon painters,
belongs to dilletantes. It has no serious factual basis,
if one discounts as such basis the isolated cases of
abuses such as are mentioned in a ukase of the Czar
Alexis Michailovich, aimed against the Holuisky icon
painters.[1 If it is possible to talk of general
----
1)
   (I. E. Sabelin. Materials for the History of Icon
      Painting. Annals (Vremennik) of Moscow Society
      of History and Antiquities, 1850 Vol. 7,
      pp. 85-86.)
----
principles of schools and periods in the history of
Western paintings considering the complete freedom and
originality of the artistic ideas of Western artists,
so much more natural is the coordination in the Byzantine-
Russian iconography classification, which is mostly of
a hieratic character. Byzantine iconography from its
first steps, allied itself with religion and served its
.

purposes. Iconography began to be looked upon as one
of the means of the religious and moral education of the
people. This point of view took such root toward the
VIII century that at the Seventh General Council the
necessity of prohibiting any kind of innovation in iconography was pointed out. One of the members of the
Council,(Deacon Epiphany) said that only the technical
side should be subject to the judgment of an artist;
whereas the composition of the icons he reserved to
the Saint Fathers (church dignitaries. Translator's note)
and he based it on ancient tradition.[1]   We have reason
----
1) *Ink.*

----

to think that the point of view of Epiphany did not represent in itself such an original phenomenon, which could
shock his contemporaries and would be in complete discord
with reality. The veneration for tradition and the imitation of antiquity, although not reaching a standardization
of icon painting that would not allow any development, had
been inculcated in artists by the previous epoch, therefore
Epiphany from this point of view expressed the opinion which

was applied in practice. It indicates the foundation on
which the possibility of the scientific coordination of
iconographic monuments is based: but he stretches this
point of view to excess, recommending repressive measures,
which were not in conformity with the real state of affairs.
It seems that this excess was noticed by the Fathers of
the Council: they did not organize the control over the
icons by the church: as a matter of fact, it did not exist,
not only at that time, but at any other time. At least
in the entire history of Byzantium, except during the epoch
of iconoclasm, which cleared and firmly established the
principle of icon worship, one does not see any sizeable
measures to that end. The church's power not only did
not offer any kind of guiding rules in iconography, but
did not even protest against innovations. At the same
time these innovations were not rare phenomena. The ex-
pansion of Christian ideas expanded iconographic cycles;
with the increase in religious festivals, new writings
and collections of writings appeared, the ideas of which
were transferred in art, even sometimes directly on the
walls of churches, in the form of mosaics. And if now we
look at some of the monuments of Byzantine antiquity from
the point of view of the conceptions already established
about sources of iconography and religious teachings in
our time, then perhaps we find in them much that is

superfluous and arbitrary, which theological thought,
roared in the severe formulas of religious teaching
can not admit. The Byzantine attitude to this question
was different. Keeping for themselves the point of
view on the icon as an object of veneration and medium
of instruction of the people, Byzantine theologians
were far from applying to each separate picture exactly
fixed measurement of religious teaching, or applying
criticism to the picture. They knew very well that the
people will not draw from iconography new dogmas and
create on this unstable foundation new heresies and
schisms: and therefore they allowed a certain degree of
freedom in this sphere, providing that iconographic
innovations did not shock the eye by flagrant ten-
dentiousness. The history of iconography from this point
of view is analogous to the history of the ecclesiastical ritual. The assemblage of Byzantine ecclesiastical
rituals was by no means created by the exact prescrip-
tions of councils or individuals, who would be occupying
themselves with the creation of complete rituals and
ceremonials and of spreading them everywhere. The number
of the ritual rules which owe their existence to Councils
is extremely limited. On the whole, history created
the ritual. The life of the church and the inward and

outward conditions of its development call forth ritual
and ecclesiastical usages, first local, which with time
gain forms exactly defined in the written set of rules
and receive the general recognition of the church. The
same thing applies to iconography. And if in spite of
the existence of definite codes, in the form of written
statutes, apparently limiting the ritual, the church
allows newly appearing rituals and even entire services,
then it also allows changes in ecclesiastical iconography.
But neither divine services nor iconography could be
considered dogmatic systems, in which the entire content
up to the most minute details is sanctioned and officially
recognized, and in which the smallest signs of private
opinion and points of view are missing. Only with time
when the tremendous work of re-examination of all our
books of divine servies rituals, iconography and so on
is finished, shall Catholics and Protestants have the
right to address themselves to these subjects as to one
of the sources of Orthodox dogma. Be that as it may,
the VII General Council set up no repressive measures
against iconography, although/veneration for tradition
expressed by Epiphany corresponded to the spirit of its
(the General Council's) definitions and general point of
view on the religious painting of that time. The church

did not support the iconographic uniformity in Byzantium

by external measures, but by the character of education

of artists, by the general and established set of concep-

tions of ecclesiastical art, and by the general principle

of conservatism of the Eastern church. It even allowed

a development, but the latter, from its inward side, was

not so much the product of personal inventiveness, as

the expression of ideas and conceptions already intro-

duced into general usage. Innovations were easily assim-

ilated. They brought forth imitations, and little by

little increased the stock of the traditional iconograph-

ical forms. Clearly the coordination of the results of

development which had such a conventional character is

entirely feasible. Eight centuries later, after the

aforementioned General Council, when Western Europe was

able to present a long succession of brilliant artistic

schools and trends, in which there was not only no visible

traces left of Byzantine influence, but even the basic

standpoint on the purposes of the art was entirely changed,

with us in Russia there was again brought forth the old

basis of veneration of tradition and of copying holy pic-

tures from the best ancient Greek and Russian examples.

The exponent of it proved to be the Council of the Hundred

Chapters. Its decision had no practical consequences,

but for us the important fact is that here is supported

the old standpoint on iconography as a subject that has

stability and precision of form. And after all, are

not Greek and Russian painters' guides the evident proof

of the same iconographical precision? They offer for

the guidance of artists, descriptions of all the most

important pictures and therefore/the possibility and the
                                 presuppose

necessity of uniformity and subordination to certain

regulations; and the monuments that have been preserved

prove with complete clearness, that the requirements

of painters' guides not only did not contradict the ac-

tual reality, but also restrained the tendencies toward

personal artistic whims, that is, they helped the purpose,

to which the Council of the Hundred Chapters aspired in

vain. If even these painters' guides, in spite of the

assurances of their introductions, do not stem from the

Byzantine epoch, at least they prove that such a stand-

point was preserved with us in the XVI-XVIII centuries.

From this point of view the Byzantine-Russian iconography

differs entirely from the Western. To appreciate this

difference correctly it is necessary to pay attention to

their fundamental principles. In some particular cases

they can sometimes approach each other, but in principle

they had already grown apart in the XIII century: in

the West, the border between the ecclesiastical and secular

iconography is destroyed; in one as in the other equally
individual thought and artists' inspiration dominate,
not being restricted by tradition: entirely new forms
are introduced in ecclesiastical iconography and their
merits are determined by means of the same criterion as
in secular art: the icon designated for the church is
treated as any other picture designated for a drawing-
room. Such a picture can carry away the emotions and the
imagination, can bring forth a feeling of enraptured
emotion and a bitter weeping, but does not conform with
the Eastern Orthodox point of view upon an icon, as one
of the edifying media and an object of religious veneration. Our ancestors drew a line between iconography and
secular painting, just as between ecclesiastical teaching and private instruction. An icon as the representation of a certain idea in certain established forms,
according to their belief, should not allow of **arbitrary**
changes. This standpoint appeared as a direct deduction
from the general point of view on the church ritual.
Guarding the ritual from innovations, our ancestors also
guarded iconography. Our contemporary point of view and
practice on these subjects are not distinguished by such
logical consistency. We have a just respect not only
toward the dogmatic and canonic, but also toward the

ritual traditions of antiquity, guard them from arbitrary
distortions, bring up questions of uniformity of ecclesiastical practice, and try to make it conform with the
old traditions; as concerns iconography, we leave it at
the complete disposal of unrecognized artists, brought
up not at all in that spirit which is required for ecclesiastical painting. It would seem as if it were a matter
which has no relation to the ecclesiastical question.
Leaving aside the question of inconsistency, the result
of this is that our iconography loses more and more its
definite character and changes into a pitiful copying of
Western pictures;the merits of its inner content are sac-
rificed to realism; the iconographic forms and compositions borrowed from the West sometimes are in direct discord with the traditions of the Eastern church, as for
instance the image not made with hands with the wreath
of thorns (the imprint of the fact of Jesus on the
napkin. Translator's note.), and the Eastern legend of
its origin; the murals in churches are placed without
any definite order, and in this way the edifying symbolism
of a church expressed by its ancient murals disappears;
even in church iconostasies the ornamentation begins to
oust the iconography. The lack of a definite point of   Page VI
view on character and purposes of church iconography,
the complete arbitrariness, the blind imitation of the

West - that is what our contemporary reality shows us.
The exceptions are rare.

So then the standpoint on the ecclesiastical iconography prevailing in antiquity gives us the basis for
considering antique monuments collectively, as an expression of a certain definite idea. Their classification on the basis of identity of forms is at the same
time the classification according to the inner content.
In the process of an archaeological work the external
classification of monuments occupies the first place;
but the final purpose of iconographical research does
not consist in this. In themselves groups of monuments
represent only the skeleton which requires inspiriting.
A definite scheme prepared by diverting the attention
from available monuments, presupposes a certain inner
content. Is it true, and where to look for the key to
the solution of the inner sense of iconographical compositions? If Byzantine iconography has always stood
in a narrow union with religion, then it is understand-
able that its forms must express definite ideas and
conceptions. Otherwise the continuous repetition of
compositions which we notice in its history would be
impossible: chance phenomena not sufficiently defined
from the point of view of their inner content, could
hardly find general recognition. In the iconographical

productions of the Byzantine artists the subjective
element occupies the second place; they tried to stay
in the sphere of ideas and conceptions of common usage,
moulding them into artistic forms. Being on the level
of contemporary knowledge, they transferred it into
iconography. It is impossible to assert that Byzantine
iconography embraces the whole complex of this knowledge:
its field is much narrower, and every attempt on our
part to fill the lack of literary monuments with the
monuments of iconography could not meet with any success.
The only thing that is true is that Byzantine artists
were inspired by the same ideas, revolved in the same
circle of thoughts and conceptions as their contempor-
aneous religious thinkers. Therefore it is possible to
compare their productions with the monuments of ancient
literature; with the help of the latter it is possible
to ascertain exactly the inner content of iconographical
compositions. The main task consists in finding these
monuments and ascertaining their real connection with
the iconographical monuments. Such monument of literature in its application to Gospel iconography, as has
already been mentioned, serves the Gospel itself first
of all: in it are given not only all basic themes of
Gospel iconography, but are even indicated some details
of the characters, types, circumstances and history of

events important in the matter of artistic creation. But
if this primary source was not always and in everything
sufficient for artists, then also it is not sufficient
for a scientific explanation of monuments of ancient
Gospel iconography. Many events are related in the Scriptures very briefly and for their artistic transmission
it was required to supplement them from other sources;
therefore, for the explanation of iconographical phenomena
of that kind it is necessary to turn to other monuments
of the written language, aside from the Scriptures.
Neither their evaluation nor even a simple enumeration
of them could be made here; it will be given in the
analyses of iconographical subjects. Here it is sufficient
to mention that these monuments are very disparate in
their character: some are exegetic, others historical,
homiletic and liturgic. Not the least place is occupied
by the monuments of apocryphal literature. They are
being insistently pointed out as a source of iconography
by many experts; we shall mention Count Uvarov, de- Vaal,
N.P. Kondakov, A.I. Kirpichnikov, E.B. Barsov, Mr. Ainalov
and Mr. Redin. Enthusiasm over them sometimes reaches
such limits that could only be explained by insufficient
acquaintance with the monuments of iconography, as for

instance, in the observations on this subject expressed
by Mr. Sakharov.[1 Within the limits of exact facts,

----

1) (Christian Reading (Christianskoie Chtenie) 1888
   No. 3-4, p. 296).

----

serious comparison of them with monuments of iconography

has its basis: it is possible to apply it in some cases

toward ancient-Byzantine monuments and particularly

toward Medieval Western and Russian of the XVII century,

when illuminated manuscripts of legends of the Passion of

Christ came into fashion with us. Nevertheless, no

matter how we regard the origin and significance of the

apocryphies, whether we consider them productions of ancient

heretics, put into circulation for the purpose of pro-

paganda of heretical errors, or a product of pious im-

agination, brought forth by the brevity of the true

Scriptures; whether we consider their content entirely an

invention of the imagination or whether we find in them

a particle of truth transmitted here partly from the true

Scriptures and partly from unwritten legends, in any case

the attitude toward them of Byzantine iconography has no

tendential character. Byzantines have not had complete

illuminated codices of apocryphal Scriptures; in any case,

we have not succeeded in finding there anything of that

description. Not one of the dogmatic errors, brought

forth in the apocryphal Scriptures, finds more or less clear reflection in Byzantine iconography. The external details of events, narrated in the true Scriptures - that is the ground on which the Byzantine iconography sometimes meets with apocryphies. But these details often repeat themselves also in the other monuments of ancient literature, which from/dogmatical point of view have nothing in common with apocryphies. The question of how this similarity originated is not yet solved: whether it can be explained by borrowing directly from apocryphies or borrowing from the most ancient legends, which authors of apocryphies also used. Some details of Gospel narratives are mentioned by ecclesiastical writers apparently earlier than the apocryphies themselves received the final version, and without any doubt, earlier than the latter were included in the index librorum prohibitorum.

Having defined the purposes and the ways of our research, we shall pass on to reviewing sources of Gospel iconography. It is necessary in the first place because many sources are not yet known to ecclesiastico-archaeological science, and appear here for the first time, and the sources, known previously to the other authors, are examined by us from a different angle; in the second place, because of using these sources for an explanation of the

history of separate iconographic subjects, we must

necessarily separate them into their component parts;

but as they are also interesting in their entirety it

is necessary to characterize them separately as com-

plete monuments, with their essential peculiarities,

occupying one or another place in the complete series of

monuments of Gospel iconography; in the third place,

a review of sources will show us the general historical

course of Gospel iconography; and finally in the fourth

place, this presents us with visible proof of the degree

of the completeness of our research.

A) The first place among the sources of Byzantine

Russian Gospel iconography should be given to the ancient

codices of illuminated Gospels. In the complete illumin-

ated Gospels there is an entire and complete iconographic

cycle of Gospel events, which we cannot find in any of

the other groups of monuments. It is only in them alone

that we find certain miracles of the Gospel, certain

parables, sermons, journeys and the like, that is, such

details to which the consecutive narrative of the Evan-
                                miniaturists
gelists led, but for the separate representation of which

on an icon or a church mosaic there was no urgent induce-

ment. But in spite of possessing this numerical

completeness, the illuminated Gospels do not contain in
their illustrations such breadth and freedom of ideas,
nor such originality of invention of subjects, as are
possible in other monuments and even in miniatures of
some manuscripts, as for instance, psalters, the homilies
of Jacobus, works of edifying character. Illuminated
manuscripts were intended not so much for private use as
for church use. Before the consciousness of miniaturists
there was ever present the text of the Gospel, inviolable
and not tolerating either abbreviations or additions,
as the main basis for determining iconographic compositions. Therefore in the illuminated Gospels even of
the XII century one can often find such simple compositions on subjects which in other monuments were at that
time exchanged for other more complicated representations.
Miniaturists of illuminated Gospels had no purpose in
completing the Gospel text by means of visible forms,
based on the other sources and in this way commenting on
the Gospel. Such tendencies, if they really took place,
would change considerably those simple iconographic schemes
which we see now in the ancient illuminated Gospels.
Actually the aims of ministurists of the Gospel were much
more modest. They were trying to relate in visual forms
only the direct and objective content of the Gospel text.

If such illustrations even could serve didactical purposes, then only as far as visualization in general re-
inforces the impression produced by a mere narrative.
But as the iconographic traditions of Byzantium under
the influence of hieratic principle were stable and defined and as not only mosaists, icon painters, and sculp-
tors, but even miniaturists developed their artistic
taste and practical usages on traditional forms, then
as a consequence, miniaturists sometimes brought into
Gospel miniatures even such details as are not mentioned
in the Gospel text, but which from ancient times were
introduced in the sphere of iconography, and repeated
according to the tradition in monuments of all kinds.
Force of habit prevailed over theoretical considerations
of literalism and exactitude and prevented strict sep-
aration of the Gospel miniatures from the monuments
of a different kind. Such deviations in the illuminated codices of Gospels are not numerous; besides, they
do not represent an exclusive phenomenon in the entire
complex of Byzantine iconography, created with the express purpose of commenting on the Gospel text. The
main role of the illuminated Gospels in the general
history of Byzantine iconography consists in the creation

anew of iconographic forms for some subjects on certain
themes of the Gospel and in this way therefore give completeness to the entire cycle of Gospel iconography.

The most ancient of the codices of illuminated
Gospels that/reached us do not go back earlier than the
have
VI century. Were these codices that are known to us the
first attempts at illuminated Gospels, or do they represent copies of originals more ancient? Many of those
pictures that were inserted in these most ancient codices
existed already in the iconography of the earlier time:
we find them already in the mosaic and sculpture of the
IV and V centuries and the historic connection between
them is without any doubt. Concerning one of these
codices - the Syrian Gospel of Rabula, it was long ago -
noted that the careless roughness and technical imperfec-
tion in the execution of its miniatures and at the same
time the artistry of composition show that the miniaturist
must have used the existing originals.[1] But did
----
1) (N.P.Kondakov. History of Byzantine Art. p. 71)
----
special codices of illuminated Gospels exist before?
Neither such monuments nor more or less direct indications
of them have reached us. The monuments of ancient literature speak on the subject indistinctly. From them we

learn about the existence in the IV - V centuries of
precious codices of the Gospel with magnificent decorations, but they do not mention directly miniature pictures
of persons and events of the Gospel. Eusebius witnesses
that the Emperor Constantine intrusted him with the preparation of the books for the churches of Constantinople,
that among their number were well written and even luxur-
iously prepared scrolls in three and four sheets.[2

[2) Vita Const. IV, 36-37. Valesii historiae eccles.
scriptores, ed. 1746, t. I.

There were probably also the Gospels; but the historian
says no word about holy pictures. John Chrysostom in the
thirty second discourse on the subject of the Gospel of
John mentioned the use by Christians, his contemporaries,
of luxurious codices of the Bible written on the magnificent material (   ) in excellent script (   ) with
golden letters (· ·   ).[3

[3) Migne Patrol, c. c.s. gr. t. LIX, col. 187.

Kedrin says that the Emperor Constantine embellished the
Gospels of the city's great church with gold and precious

stones.[4   But these decorations evidently refer to the

----

4) *....*

Corp. script. hist. byzant. Ed. Nieburii. Georgius
Cedrenus t. I p. 517.

----

coverings of the Gospels; the same decorations are in

mind in the tale about the Emperor Zeno, who honored

in the same way the codex which was found on the breast

of the Apostle Barnabas in the year 485.[5   About Theo-

----

5) Ciampini Vet. monim. t. I. p. 132.

----

dosius Junior it was known that he was a good calligraphist.[6

----

6) Muralt Chronogr. byzant. t. I p. 16.

In general the art of calligraphy is a matter incontrovert-

ible not only in the IV and V centuries but also for the

III century. It is known also that valuable codices of

the Gospels were preserved in elegant caskets and were ven-

erated.[7   Monuments of miniature painting before the VI

----

7) Facts: Kraus Real-Encyclopaedie der christl. Alter-
    thümer I, 457.

----

century have also reached us, but these miniatures have the

character of antiquity; the basis for them was prepared by

the earlier history of art, which one could not say in
the same measure in regard to the illumination of the Gospel. A specifically Christian creation was required for
the latter to a much greater degree than for instance for
the illumination of the Iliad, the works of Virgil and
even the Book of Genesis, illuminated manuscripts of which
go back earlier than the VI century. And therefore if the
illuminated Gospels preserved for us are copies, still
their originals are not far from them in time. The
archaeological facts do not allow of placing the beginning
of the illuminated Gospels earlier than the V and even the
VI centuries. The symbolic cycle of Christian pictures
was developed and the transition from Greco-Roman art to
original Christian art was marked in the first three centuries of Christianity; the artistic energy of the IV
and V centuries was directed to the development of main
types and subjects in the Christian spirit: Christian
art started the new trend and although there is a certain
hesitation and inconsistency in the handling of antique
Christian forms, it is clear that a turn back was impossible; the fundamental aims of the art are marked
firmly. The hesitation was finished in the VI century;
Christian art developed and grew strong. If one compares
the Ravennate mosaics of the V century (the baptisteries
of the church of Galla Placida) with the mosaics of the

the VI century (of the Church of Appollinaris Nuovo and

Vitali), then one will note what a decisive step was

taken by the art in the new direction during the course

of one century: the same one can see in the other suff-

iciently numerous monuments of that time. The con-

sciousness of artistic strength and the skill of handling

Christian themes, a large reserve of ready material, could Page IX

inspire Byzantine artists for the great work of illumination

of the entire Gospel. For such work there was necessary

not only knowledge of traditional forms, but creative en-

ergy and as a necessary condition of success, a deep pene-

tration into the essence of the Gospel. Such a problem

could not be solved in all its minutest details in a short

time, and by the efforts of a single person; for that,

more than one century was required: but it is important

that in the V and VI centuries such a strong basis for this

work was laid, that it determined its further course. If

one compares illuminated codices, which stand not far from

the two opposite poles in the history of Byzantine art,

namely codices of the VI century from one side, and of

the XII century from the other, and these later with the

latest codices of the XVI and XVII centuries, then it is

evident that the illuminated Gospels had a certain develop-

ment, although conventional, as was noted before. The

artistic and theological thought of the Gospel miniaturists, subordinated necessarily to the requirements of
the time, could not during the course of several centuries be limited by those iconographic forms which were
given in the Gospels of the VI century. The rigidity of
form, the complete lack of creative activity, mechanical
imitation, also pretentious tendency toward innovation
and didacticism without sufficient talent and knowledge
are the signs of the decadence of art; but the state of
affairs in Byzantium in the epoch of the VI - XII centuries was different. Here were present not only talents
but ready impulses, for art in the general character of
civilization. Let us take for granted that Greek literature had declined considerably already by the VI century, but still it existed and had many of such features
as could directly stimulate the development of predilec-
tion for illuminated gospels. The edifying and partly
legendary character of literature, transferring thought
and imagination into the sphere of magic, recalling the
pictures of paradise and hell, excited interest particularly toward that part of the Gospel where the miracles
produced by the Savior are narrated: and in fact that
part of the Byzantine Gospel is distinguished by the
particular abundance of the illustrations. A dry and

abstract tendency in literature is a bad fellow traveller
of art. But admitting a development in illuminated Gospels, it is necessary to mention its character. The
basic types and subjects do not undergo a considerable
change according to a personal whim of artists; the
changes in them concern only details: once established
types are being introduced into new iconographical combinations, new subjects are created, some new types are
defined. But new types and subjects with few exceptions
are created not without influence of the above mentioned
more important types and subjects; therefore here we
see not so much an original creation as an adaptation
of ready basic forms for the expression of new ideas.
Analysis of the monuments preserved for us will show us
more exactly the relationship between the most ancient
and the most recent illuminated Gospels. The Byzantine
codices that have reached us are not numerous: a part
of them belongs to the VI century but the greatest part
to the X and XII centuries. The lacuna in the monuments
at hand coincides with the epoch of iconoclasm; nevertheless, the iconoclastic movement cannot be accepted as
the sole reason for the lack of monuments. The main part
of the monuments have perished without a trace, but the
others are not yet known. Their discovery, which have

occurred oftener and oftener in modern times, makes us
think that with time their number will increase considerably. It is impossible that in the course of an entire
millenium in Buzantium, which is rich in all respects,
there could appear the some two or three tens of illuminated Gospels which we have now. And there is no doubt
that the amount of the monuments at hand is not complete:
some of them, according to all indications, are copies of
the more ancient originals, the latter being still missing.

      The most ancient of the Greek illuminated Gospels
has
that/reached us is the Rossano Codex, which was found by
Gebhardt and Harnack in the small Calabrian town of Rossano,
where, as is known, the Greek ritual and the Greek language
were retained until the XV century in the divine service.
It was written on parchment with silver, and according to
the credible deduction of the learned editors, in the VI
century,[1 but according to the conclusion of Mr. Usov,

[1) Gebhardt u. A. Harnack Evangel. codex graecus purpur.
rossan. litteris argenteis sexto ut videtur saeculo
scriptus picturisque ornatus. Leipzig 1880.

----

in the year 527. [2 Whether this Gospel appeared in lower

[2)The proceedings of the Moscow Archaeological Society
1881 Vol. IX.

Egypt, as Mr. Usov supposed, or in some other place, in
any case the character of its miniatures give us ground
to place it at the head of illuminated Gospels. Unfortunately the preserved codex is not complete; only two
Gospels of Matthew and Mark are included in it. The miniatures are placed not in the text of the manuscript and
not among the canons of Eusebius, which are missing here,
but on the first fly leaves before the Gospel of Matthew.
In this latter circumstance, according to our opinion,
lies one of the signs of the antiquity of the manuscript:
here one does not yet see that meticulousness with which
the later miniaturists placed their miniatures directly Page X
to the corresponding text and not seldom to follow more
exactly the text, they separate subjects into their component parts, placing them separately, and in that way
they sacrifice to punctiliousness the artistic completeness of the pictures. Here miniatures did not succeed in
blending with the text, and themselves represent one of
the most important parts of the codex. Their style also
bears witness to their great antiquity: one notices in
the compositions of the miniatures, in the types and in
the garments, the traces of antiquo-Christian art: the
classical figure of Pilate, the naked figure of the one
who fell among thieves, showing skill of reproduction of

the human body, reared on the study of sculpture, animals
and birds recalling Greco-Roman ornamentation, beautiful
figures of the wise and foolish virgins, a mountain with
four paradise rivers are a clear echo of the art of the
catacomb period - all these are the signs of an epoch not
far from the first centuries of Christianity. At the same
time the type of the Savior with the beard, Byzantine
garments with tablions and diadems in the pictures of the
prophet David, the reproduction of the Eucharist as the
distribution of holy bread and a chalice, a lack of schooling in the pictures of the Savior, praying in the Garden of
Gethsemane and reclining at the Last Supper, and in the
poses of the Apostles receiving communion and the bound
thief, give us the vision of the approach of the new epoch
in the history of art. The first half of the VI century
is the most appropriate time for the production of such
miniatures. In the part of the codex that has been pres-

PICTURE
Caption. The Wise and Foolish Virgins. From
the Rossano Gospel.

erved there are 18 pictures referring to different events
of the Gospel, and 40 pictures of the prophets. They are
placed on the sheets 1 to 4 on 7 and 8 in that order as is
shown on the table, arranged by us according to the description of Hebhardt and Harnack. The publishers of the codex

David Joshua David Isaiah	Raising of Lazarus	Sheet 1 a.
David Zachariah David Malachi (1	Entry of Jesus Christ into Jerusalem	Sheet 1 b. Sheet 2 a
David Joshua David Isaiah	Driving of the money- changers out of the temple	Sheet 2 a.
David David David Joshua	The wise and foolish virgins	Sheet 2 b Sheet 3 a
David David David Zephaniah	The Last Supper and washing of the feet	Sheet 3 a
David Moses David Isaiah	The Eucharist (bread)	Sheet 3 b Sheet 4 a
Moses David David Solomon	The Eucharist (wine)	Sheet 4 a
David David Jonah Micah	The Prayer of Jesus Christ in the Garden of Gethsemane	Sheet 4 b Sheet 7 a
David Sirach David Isaiah	The healing of the blind in two instances	Sheet 7 a
David Micah David Sirach	The parable of the Good Samaritan (in two instances)	Sheet 7 b Sheet 8 a
Judas returning money to the Chief Priests The death of Judas	Jesus Christ before Pilate	Sheet 8 a
Jesus Christ and Barabbas	Judeans before Pilate	Sheet 8 b

David; but judging by the sign on the scroll (and Our Lord will be the king of

had reason to mention that 1) the pages with the pictures
are bound incorrectly, the chronological sequence of Gospel events required that the seventh page should be placed
before the first because the healing of the blind and the
parable of the Good Samaritan preceded the raising of
Lazarus from the dead; in the case of such juxtaposition,
page eight would have its natural place after page four;
2) that some pages with the miniatures are lost. Presupposing that the miniatures must represent something
complete in themselves, the publishers think that the
miniaturist illustrated either the entire Gospel or only
the Passion of Our Lord; but as here one finds pictures
which have no relation to the Passion, such as the healing of the blind and the parable of the Good Samaritan,
then evidently the first supposition is more correct.
It is difficult to say how much the Gospel was illustrated;
according to the note of the publishers, it is only true
that the miniaturist could not begin from the healing of
the blind; it is also doubtful that in accordance with
the usual order of miniatures, the parable of the Good
Samaritan could be placed next to the raising from the
dead of Lazarus, the judgment of Pilate next to the prayer

and finished cycle of the Passion of Our Lord; the whole
aim of the miniaturist consisted only in this. As the
determining basis for the miniaturist there served the
text not of the original Gospels, but the apocryphic
Gospel of Nicodemus; this fact, according to the opinion
of Mr. Usov, explains not only the general composition
of the miniatures of the Rossano Codex, but also the
details of its iconographic subjects. This supposition
is not entirely acceptable from the external point of
view. A miniaturist predestined his pictures for the
canonic Gospels and he has their text at hand; what necessity was there to turn to an apocryphy? We do not deny
that in the complete history of Byzantine-Russian iconography apocryphies have their significance: when an
artist painted an icon, or murals of a church, he could
admit an apocryphal detail in addition to the brief narrative of the original Gospel, even introduce a whole series
of subjects, based on the apocryphal legend; while in the
miniatures of the canonic Gospel, the whole series of
apocryphic subjects is quite impossible. The supposition
of the apocryphic basis in this case would compel us to
accept that the miniaturist preparing the miniatures for
canonic Gospels neglected the connection of events given
in these Gospels and preferred the one in accordance with
the apocryphy, that is, he introduced in the cycle planned

the healing of the blind, the raising from the dead of
Lazarus, the parable of the wise and foolish virgins only
because in the apocryphy these events are connected with
the judgment of Pilate and omitted the Resurrection of
Christ solely on the ground that it is not mentioned in
the apocryphy. Only a man contaminated by the thought
of preference for the apocryphy as against the original
Gospels could adopt such manner of illustration; but in
such a case it would be more expedient to affix his
illustrations to the text of the apocryphy, but not to
the original Gospel. Besides, it should be noticed that
Mr. Usov in adapting the miniatures to the text of the
apocryphy allows some forced explanations. Remarking
that the parable of the Samaritan and the driving out of
the money changers are not mentioned in the apocryphy and
yet are among the miniatures of the codex, he supposes
that the first miniature represents an idea of the bene-
ficence of Jesus Christ in accordance with the narrative
of the apocryphy about the healing of a cripple and
leper and the second points to that part of the apocryphy
where the destruction of the temple is mentioned. It
is a strange way of illustrating! In addition to that,
asserting the connection of these miniatures with the
Judgment of Pilate according to the apocryphy. Mr. Usov,

for reasons not entirely comprehensible, severed this
connection. The sequence required that the miniatures
of the healing of the blind and parables of the Samaritan
remained beside the judgment of Pilate as it is in the
actual placing of the miniatures while he transposed them
to the beginning and placed them before the raising from
the dead of Lazarus and the entrance into Jerusalem,
separating them from the Judgment also by the pictures
of the Last Supper and the washing of the feet! This has
its sense only in the presupposing of chronological sequence
of the pictures in the original Gospels but not in the
apocryphy. The connection of the iconographical details
in the pictures of the manuscript under consideration
with the Gospel of Nicodemus is exaggerated in the ex-
position of Mr. Usov and is not firmly founded: he sees
the influence of the apocryphy in the picture of the
driving of the money changers out of the Temple (pp. 44-45)
while there is nothing that refers directly to this event
in the source mentioned, and the author himself evidently
had doubts concerning the truth of this conjuncture, when
a little farther on he remarked that for explanation of
this miniature acquaintance with the canonic Gospels is
enough. The author showed the same hesitation, to the
point of inconsistency, also in the explanation of the

picture of the entry of Jesus Christ into Jerusalem,
first acknowledging in it the influence of the apocryphy
and then remarking that it could be explained also without the apocryphy. But we will ignore the details
which have no important significance and turn our attention to the further course of thought of Mr. Usov in
explaining the whole. Establishing the connection of
the miniatures of the Rossano Gospel with the apocryphy,
Mr. Usov introduces here one arbitrating principle which
impairs unity and sequence. Remarking that the choice
of subjects was suggested here by the apocryphic Gospel
of Nicodemus, the author evidently noticed the embarrass-
ing situation in which he put the miniaturist and hast-
ened to justify him, but unsuccessfully. In a special
chapter, dedicated to analyzing the whole cycle of miniatures and their relation to the four Gospels, he pays
attention to the festivals and Gospel readings in the
order of the church calendar, and in them he finds a
basis why the artist limited himself by such a comparatively small cycle of pictures (p. 67 and the following).
Now it appears that the determining factor in this case
was the memorial observance of the Orthodox church in
the Passion Week and namely: forty days were concluded
by Palm Saturday and the Passion Week begins with the

observance of Palm Sunday; the entry of Jesus Christ
into Jerusalem is remembered in the "Vay" week; during
the Mass on Monday of the Passion Week the Gospel of
Matthew XXI, 18-43 is read. In it is brought to memory
the discourse of Jesus Christ after the driving of the
money changers from the Temple; on Tuesday - the parable
about the ten virgins; on Wednesday it is the supper
in the house of Simon the Leper: on Thursday it is the
Washing of the Feet, the Last Supper, the prayer in the
Garden of Gethsemane and the Betrayal of Judas; on
Friday the Passion of Our Lord and the judgment of
Pilate. These memories of the Passion Week are supposed
to be expressed in the miniatures of the Rossano codex.
The conformity here without any doubt exists; but the
fact of the matter is that the church memories themselves
are related by the author not exactly, but with a certain
adaptation to the existing complex of miniatures. First
of all, for the attainment of his aim the author should
determine the antiquity of these memories more exactly,
not limiting himself by the general reference to the antiquity of the divine service books: this is important,
because some of these memories could appear after the VI
century, when the Rossano codex was written and if only
for this one reason could not be used for this purpose.

As an instance, we shall point out the fact that according
to monuments of ancient Slavonic literature, the divine
service derived directly from the Greek, and there has
not been prescribed any reading of the Gospel on the Monday
Mass;[1 therefore the deduction based on this Gospel

----

1) A.A.Dmitrievsky. Divine Service in the Russian Church
   in the XVI century p. 208.

----

about the memories of this day are not valid. At present
on Passion Monday there are remembered not the driving of
the moneychangers out of the temple and not the discourse
which followed this event, but the chaste Joseph, the
prototype of Christ who was sold into Egypt, and the
barren fig tree representing the human soul, which does
not give good fruit. Then Mr. Usov connects with Passion
Wednesday the picture of the Last Supper of Jesus Christ
with his disciples, presented according to the historical
conception in the reclining around the table, which is
sigma-shaped [2 and he sees in that picture the supper   Page XIII

----

2) Gebhardt u. Harnack Taf. VIII.

----

in the house of Simon the leper; but he forgets that the
essential feature of the picture of the supper in the
house of Simon, according to the monuments of Byzantine

iconography, is a woman, who anointed Jesus Christ with
ointment which we do not find in the picture that we
are considering. We have here in accordance with all
iconographical signs, a picture of the Last Supper,
which is indicated also by the Washing of the Feet placed
beside it on the same sheet. Any doubt produced by the
inexactitude of the above explanations is transformed
into the complete certitude of the invalidity of the
principle if we pay attention to the following. In the
succession of the memories of the Passion Week there are
no memories relating to the parable of the Good Samaritan
and the healing of the blind. For their explanation the
author goes beyond the limits of the set cycle of memories and turns toward the fourth and the first weeks
of Lent. But in the hymns of the fourth week there is
only/indirect hint of this parable, when the soul of a
repentant sinner is compared to the man who fell among
thieves. The miniaturist of the Codex Rossanensis, as
far as one can judge it by the fragments of his work
preserved, had not the slightest inclination to transfer
into miniatures lyric similes of that kind; such a trend
in an artist of the VI century would be an anachronism
from the point of view of the history of art. In the
divine service of the Saturday of the first week of
Lent to which Mr. Usov refers for the explanation of the

picture of the healing of the blind there is not the
slightest indication of this miracle; in the Gospel of
the day (the Gospel according to Mark v. 10) (Translator's Note:- This incident is related in Mark, Chapter 3, verse 5.) there is narrated in the first place,
not two healings, as Mr. Usov says, but one; in the
second place, this healing is not of a blind man but a
man with a withered hand, and therefore has no relation
to our miniature. On the same day, according to the
rules [1 there is prescribed the reading of a different
Gospel of John (v. 52), but it does not refer to the

[1) Tipikon, publ. 1867, p. 423.
----
healing of the blind. The supposition that in antiquity
the first week of Lent was the week of the blind has
positively no basis, if one does not take into consideration its name recorded in the well-known Sinai canon
as a week of fonts, (𝘩𝘶𝘪𝘓   ), indicating probably
the ancient custom of the pre-Easter baptism but not
the Siloam font. Clearly the miniatures of the Rossano
Codex do not fit into those limits into which their in-
terpreter wishes to squeeze them. The supposed complete
cycle of the Passion of Our Lord as represented in the

present content of the miniatures is at the same time too
narrow and too wide; it is in any case not complete. It
is narrow because it does not include in it the picture
of the crucifixion and the resurrection of the Savior;
it is wide because there are miniatures there which do
not refer to the Passion of our Lord. The lack of the
crucifixion Mr.Usov explains by reference to the fact that
the ancient Christians avoided reproducing it. In general
it is correct, but in this case the significance of this
reference is weakened by the special purpose of the miniaturist: if he wished to present exactly the events of
the Passion of Our Lord, then the omission of the crucifixion appears to be incomprehensible; so much more so
that at the time of the preparation of the manuscript the
crucifixion was already known in artistic usage. Such a
cycle of pictures would represent a phenomenon without
example in the series of Byzantine monuments; in such form
it actually does not appear in a single Byzantine illuminated Gospel.

The miniatures of the Codex Rossanensis comprise
disjecta membra of something complete. Their completeness is broken by the loss of several sheets. The miniaturist had no intention of illuminating separately the
text of each Evangelist; his purpose was to give the

succession of pictures, referring to Gospel history in
general. In view of this he placed all miniatures together before the Gospel of Matthew, which place they
occupy until now. It is impossible to represent the
matter so that some of these miniatures refer to the
text of the Gospel of Matthew, others of Mark and so on;
the pictures of the healing of the blind and the parable
of the Good Samaritan do not allow of it. They are placed
on the same sheet, whereas the narratives about these
events belong to different Evangelists - John and Luke.
The same method of illustration we find also in other
codices of the psalter, the discourses of Gregory the
Theologian (Theologus) and some illustrated Gospels
(the Gospel of Rabula, the Armenian Gospel of the Ech-
miadzin library,(2 the Syrian Gospel in the Paris National

----

2) Described by Count A. S. Uvarov in the Proceedings of
   the V Archaeological Congress, pp. 352-357.

Library No. 33. A particularly interesting peculiarity
of the illuminations of the Rossano Gospel is pictures of
prophets together with the pictures of the New Testament.
In the conscience of the miniaturist the New and the Old
Testaments were inseparably bound up with one another.
Some basis for such a connection is given directly in the

Gospel text, where there are often quoted the prophesies
of the Old Testament prophets concerning the New Testament; but the miniaturist goes in this case even further;
he brings forth also such prophesies as are not mentioned
in the Gospel, as one can see from our table; therefore
he introduces into the illumination a certain element of Page XIV
theological interpretation, although he does not give it
any iconographical development. It would be possible to
determine exactly even the character itself of this
exegesis if we knew the signs on the scrolls of the
prophets; unfortunately they were left undeciphered. The
truth of the matter is only that these prophesies refer
directly to those pictures near which they are placed.
This is proved not only by the fact of their outward
placing and by analogy with the other monuments of Byzantine iconography, but also by the remaining signs on the
scrolls of the four prophets, belonging to the picture of
the entry of Jesus Christ into Jerusalem: on the scroll
of the first prophet there is written (ֵ ֶ ֵ

) (Psalm CXVII, 26);on the second

(

(Zachariah IX, 9); on the third (

Psalm VIII, 3); on the fourth (

(Zachariah XIV, 9). It is clear that all these prophecies
refer to the royal entry of Jesus Christ into Jerusalem.

From the VI century we must pass directly to the
X - XII centuries. The lack of monuments of the intermediate
period does not allow us to follow step by step the
beginnings and the change of versions of the illuminated
Gospels: but from the last three centuries the represen-
tatives of several groups of such Gospels have reached us.
These prototypes must go back to more ancient times. In
distinction to the Codex Rossanensis all miniatures in
these Gospels are nearer to the text by their placing;
but the volume of their illuminations is not equal: in
some, the most simple, only four events are illustrated -
one from each Evangelist, or only the festival Gospel readings at the end of each codex; in the others, several of
the most remarkable events from each of the Evangelists;
in the third ones, the most complete, all the most important and even secondary events of the Gospel. From the
same period we have a multitude of Gospels with pictures
of the Evangelists only and a few Syrian, Coptic and

Armenian, the illumination of which originated in the
same Byzantium. In our characterization of these monuments we shall pursue the following order of the groups.

I. To the first group we relate those Gospels
in which all iconographical content consists only of
four, five and six miniatures. They serve in most cases
as the frontispieces of the Gospels or vignettes. Their
choice was made according to the peculiarities of the
content of the Gospels and preference is given to the
themes that have the closest connection to the festivals
of the church. To this group belong 1) The Greek Gospel
of the National Library in Paris of the XI century (No.75).
Before the Gospel of Matthew the picture of the Nativity
is placed (sheet 1); before the Gospel of Mark the baptism of Jesus Christ (sheet 95); before the Gospel of Luke -
the Annunciation of the Holy Virgin (sheet 153); before
the Gospel of John - the Resurrection (sheet 255). Bordier
remarked correctly that all these pictures are excellently
drawn and show forceful expression in movements and countenances [1]. But from our point of view the composition

----

[1] Description des peintures et autres ornements contenus
dans les manuscr. grecs de la bibl. nationale par Henri
Bordier, Paris, 1883, p. 137.

----

itself of these pictures deserves special attention: here

the miniaturist does not limit his representation by
the outward details of events, but gives them an ideal-
istic shading: in the pictures of the baptism and
resurrection he introduces the picture of sky with open
gates, in the picture of the Nativity the countenances of
angels glorifying the newly born Savior.

2) The Gospel of the Vatican Library of the year
(No. 2 Urbin.). As proof of the time of its origin there
serves, besides a notation, the excellent miniature on
sheet 19: the Savior is represented on the throne in a
purple tunic and a light blue himation; standing behind
him are two female figures in magnificent golden mantels
with crowns and unbound hair with their hands on his
shoulders; one of them to the right of the onlooker is
a personification of (;..'
the other to the left is (:..'.
The Savior is laying his hands upon the two standing lower,
The Emperors Alexius and John Commenus, dressed in the
imperial golden garments and diadems with the pendants:
the Emperors hold labara in their right hands and scrolls
in their left (2. The abovementioned personifications refer
----
2) On one of the first sheets of the manuscript is written
(   ), on the other a dedication to the Emperor
John Commenus. The miniatures are published by Agincourt
(Sammlung der Denkmäler d.Malerei Taf.LIX.) Alexius Commenus
died in 1118; before his death John ascended the Byzantine
throne (Lebeau Hist. du Bas-Empire t. XV, p.473 etc.). Perhaps
the manuscript was started during the reign of Alexius and

first of all to the Savior, in whose person are united

mercy and truth: further to the Emperors, as the ex-

pression of the most important qualities required by

the imperial title. There are four miniatures/before
of the Gospel content:

the Gospel of Matthew - the Nativity; before the Gospel

of Mark the baptism of Jesus Christ, before the Gospel

of Luke - the birth of John the Baptist (analogous to   Page XV

the Nativity of Christ before the Gospel of Matthew);

before the Gospel of John - the resurrection of Jesus

Christ. Besides that there are three Evangelists:

Matthew (writing in Greek), Luke and John. In the com-

position of the miniature we find the same traces of

idealization as in the previous codex.[1]

----

[1] In the beginning of the manuscript there are placed
excerpts from the chronicle concerning the year of
the birth of Jesus Christ, and excerpts from the
chronicle of Hippolyte of Thebes, also of Chrysostom
(concerning the Gospel of Matthew) and of Origen;
also the epigrams pertaining to all the four Gospels.

----

3) Vatican Gospel of the XI - XII centuries

(Palat. gr. No. 189)[2] with four Evangelists and four

----

[2] A brief description of the manuscript: Stevenson
Bibliotheca apostol. vatic. I. 96.

----

pictures of Gospel events as in the previous codex. The

format of the manuscript is very small (in 16mo), and

therefore the figures are also very minute; iconographic

themes are not developed, but only sketched in general.

The coloring is sufficiently fresh. To the same group

belongs also 4) The Greek Gospel of the XI - XII centuries

belonging to the Moscow Synod Biblioteck (No. 519) with

the pictures of the Nativity, baptism of Jesus Christ

and Annunciation of the Mother of God and 5) the Georgian

Gospel of the Imperial Public Library (No. 298) with

the same pictures and also the laying of Jesus Christ

into the tomb, the crucifixion and the transfiguration

(John). This method of illustration was also used in

the Russian monuments of the later period, although with

some differences. 6) In the Gospel of the Ipatievsky

Monastery of the year 1603 (No.1) before every Evangel

a special sheet of the miniature is placed but in each

of them several pictures are to be found: before the

Gospel of Matthew - the genealogy of Jesus Christ, the

Nativity, the slaying of the first-born, the flight into

Egypt and the adoration of the Magi: before Mark - the

Sermon of John the Forerunner, the baptism and the

temptation of Jesus Christ, the miracle of the loaves

and fishes, the transfiguration, the supper in the house

of Simon the Leper, the Last Supper, the descent from the

cross and the laying into the tomb; before Luke - the

birth of John the Baptist, the Annunciation, the circumcision and the medallion pictures of the ancestors of
Jesus Christ; before John - the Holy Trinity, the wedding
in Cana, the driving of the money-changers out of the
temple in Jerusalem, the discourse of Jesus Christ with
Nicodemus and the Samaritan woman, the healing of the
paralytic, the appearance of Jesus Christ to his disciples
on the Lake of Tiberias, the healing of the blind and
the raising from the dead of Lazarus. Besides this
already fairly wide and well-chosen cycle of pictures
on the front sheets, at the end of the Gospel there is
also a series of pictures appended, referring to the
history of the Passion of the Savior, beginning from the
Last Supper and ending with the ascension of Jesus Christ
to heaven. In this last series of pictures we have one
of the most ancient examples in Russia of the special
illustration of the Passion of Our Lord. From the artistic point of view the miniatures are very close to
painting in the academic sense, which is quite natural
in the Russian monument of the XVII century. 7-8) Two
                                        -Iversky
Four-Gospels - one at the Athos/Monastery, of the XI
century (No.1) and the other Athos-Panteleimonov Monastery of the XII century (No.2) have no miniatures at all
in the basic text; but placed at the end of these codices

the Gospel readings for the most important festivals are
decorated with pictures. In the first of them we find
the pictures of the Nativity of Christ, the baptism, the
transfiguration and Assumption of Our Lady done in deli-
cate colors on a golden background. The second consists
of a considerable number of pictures, related not only
to the direct content of the festival readings of the
Gospel but as well to the history of Our Lady, also separate pictures of the saints, excellent, illuminated
letters with minute pictures of Gospel events and persons inserted in them, and vignettes. The pictures of   Page XVI
the festivals are remarkable on account of their iconographic details: the elevation of the Cross (sheet 189
on the reverse) - the patriarch is dressed in a phelonion
with short hair, with a six-pointed cross in his hands,
without an omophorion; standing beside the patriarch,
clerics are dressed in short phelonions with tonsures
on the tops of their heads. Presentations of the Virgin
into the temple are pictured in two separate moments:
the Mother of God at the age of 9-10 years old being ac-
companied by virgins with their hair unbound and with
candles in their hands is on the way to the temple; she
is all concentrated on the thought of the greatness of
the task awaiting her; she is extending her hands toward
the temple and is lifting up her eyes. Iochim and Anna

are surprised by the conduct of the Mother of God. The
event, as one can see, is presented in idealized form
and this trend is expressed mainly in the Holy Virgin -
not a child as one would expect according to the tradition about the presentation of the Holy Virgin in the
temple, but a person, entirely conscious of her high
predestination. b) On the next picture the Holy Virgin
is standing before the chief priest; here also on the
second plane she is partaking of food from an angel.
The apparition of the angel to the Bethlehem shepherds
is an excellent and lively picture in which the expression of the effect on the shepherds produced by the
angels' tidings is introduced in an idyllic scene.[1

[1) See the detailed description and explanation below.

The Nativity of Christ is done according to the usual
pattern used for icon-painting "Glory to God in the
Highest", with the angels and shepherds. The baptism
of Jesus Christ has interesting iconographical details.
The purification. The Annunciation of the Holy Virgin
according to the well-known iconographical pattern
with the handiwork - one of the best Byzantine representations of this kind. On the pattern of this miniature

is the representation of the appearance of the Angel
Zachary (sheet 243), and on the pattern of the Nativity
of Christ is the birth of John the Baptist (sheet 243
on the reverse). The transfiguration of Our Lord is
presented in two moments (sheet 252 and on the reverse
side). Jesus Christ with his disciples on the way to the
Mount of Tabor and the Transfiguration itself. The
dividing of the subjects into two parts is one of the
peculiarities of this Gospel. All miniatures are done
very assiduously and with a skilled hand, and are distinguished by the freshness of their colors and are well-
preserved.   9) Vatican Gospel of the XII century
                                          the
(Vat. gr. No. 1156). In its text except for/four Evangelists there is only one picture, the Ascension of
Our Lord; but at the end among the festival readings their
number is quite considerable. Here on one sheet before
the festival readings of the Gospel there is presented
the whole series of miniatures illustrating the Passion
of the Savior: the prayer in the Garden of Gethsemane,
the kiss of Judas, Jesus on the way to trial, the crucifixion, the entombment and the resurrection.[2 This is
----
2) Published by Agincourt: Taf. LVII.
----
one of the first experiments of separating the Passion

from the other Gospel pictures in the monuments of Byzan-

tium. Farther in the calendar order we find a multitude

of separate pictures of saints which together with the

Vatican mynology could provide extensive material for

the examination of our icon painter's guide. We also

find here not a few pictures of festivals: The birth of

Our Lady, the Adoration of the holy cross,[3 the elevation

of the Cross, the presentation of the Holy Virgin in the

[3) Four pictures under the dates of the 10th, 11th, 12th
and 13th of September. Here one sees the reflection
of the divine service in accordance with the ancient
regulations of the Great Church, according to which
the holy cross was taken from the Czar's chambers into
the church on the 10th of September and was left there
until the 14th for the worshipping of the faithful
(I. D. Mansvietov.The Statute of the Church p. 153).
On these miniatures the cross is presented on an altar
(lectern); on one side af x putxixxxx there are standing a patriarch with a nimbus, with a censer in his
hands, and bishops, and on the other people worshipping
the cross.
----

temple. The events of the Nativity of Christ are ex-

pressed particularly in detail: the census of the people

in Bethlehem, the Nativity of Christ, the adoration of

the Magi and their departure, the flight into Egypt,

Herod awaiting the return of the Magis, the appearance

of the angel to Joseph, the circumcision of Our Lord,

the shepherds glorifying Our Lord, the twelve-year-old

Jesus in the temple, the baptism and the transfiguration

of Our Lord. The slavish following of the text of the

Gospel by the miniaturist and the trend toward realism

in the picture of the laying into the tomb - holy women

are wringing their hands, the angels are weeping, are

the signs of the decadence of Byzantine art. In the same

group one should include a fragment of the Greek weekly

Gospel in the Imperial Public Library (No. 21). [4 Only

[4) A description by Bishop Amphilochyin. About miniatures and decorations in the Greek Manuscript of the
Imperial Public Library. Moscow, 1870.

----

a few separate sheets are preserved from the codex. The

time of its origin is a riddle. Muralt places it in the

VII - VIII century, [5 N. P. Kondakov sees here the signs

[5) Catal. des manuscr. gr. de bibl. imper. pub. p. 13.

----

of VII - VIII centuries; and also X - XI centuries. [6

[6) History of Byzantine Art. pp. 131-133.

According to the paleographic signs this fragment be-

longs to the X - XI centuries; but in its miniatures we

find features actually belonging to different epochs.

Some of these miniatures by their style and composition

- 64 -   Page XVI

are nearer to the most ancient monuments of the VII - VIII

centuries; others to the X - XI centuries. The picture

of the wedding in Cana is an example of the former kind:

the Savior in the scene of the transformation of the

water into wine appears in the same pose with a staff

as in the scene of the miracle of the loaves and fishes: Page XVII

the scene is realistic and lively; the picture of the

Last Supper which is drawn according to the historical

pattern has the same characteristic; but the descent

into hell and the descent of the Holy Spirit on the

apostles resemble the latest composition of the IX - X

centuries.[1 It is possible to explain this difference

[1) The details will be given in the proper place. As to
the artistic style, see the cited works of N.P.Kondakov.

----

in character by the supposition that the miniaturist of

the X - XI centuries copied from the most ancient ex-

amples of the illuminated Gospel: but he did not keep

everywhere the style of the original: in some miniatures

he is an exact copyist, in others he changes and even

introduces some new miniatures, guiding himself by the

artistic examples of his own period.

II. A special group of four Gospels comprises
the codices in which the text of the Gospel is illustrated
right through. This group is the largest and the most
interesting from the iconographical point of view. Here
the miniatures are blended with the text and serve as
the most important help for its study. Among them some
are brief and the others are extensive. It is impossible
to determine the exact differences in the general trend
of these miniatures, although some of them from this
point of view have their own peculiarities. Let us
consider first the Gospels illuminated scantily.

1) The Gospel of the National Library in Paris of the X
century (No. 64).[2 Its illumination has a rather peculiar

----

2) Concerning its ornamentation see "History of Byzantine
Art" N.P.Kondakov p. 250, compare Bordier pl. 105.

----

character. The picture of the Evangelist Matthew precedes the Gospel of this Evangelist. Farther, the
beginning of the Gospel, namely the genealogy of Jesus
Christ, is divided from the other text, as a separate
division and it is illuminated: here we see the ancestors
of Jesus Christ in two separate miniatures: three old men
and a young man (sheet 10); their features do not possess
a sufficient definiteness and therefore it is impossible

to recognise them: all of them are draped in the same long

garments; the poses are majestic. In the end of the

genealogy, two kings are represented: David and Solomon[3

[3) According to Bordier they are Solomon and Rehoboam
(p. 105).

----

in Byzantine Diadems, Mother of God and Joseph. Labart

in his history of applied art supposes that the miniatur-

ist representing two kings - the ancestors of Jesus Christ,

had in mind two Byzantime emperors, reigning at that time,

Romanus Lecapenus and Constantine (Porphyrogenetus)

(919-944) and that in this detail we find a hint as to

the time of the writing of the codex.[4 This supposition

[4) Labarte Hist. des arts industr. t. 1, p. 67;III, p. 53.
Album p. LXXXIII, of. Bordier, pl. 105.

----

is very improbable. There is no doubt that the Byzantine

PICTURE

Caption. 5. Annunciation of the Holy Mother
of God. Gospel of Athos Panteleimon
Monastery No.2.

robes of David and Solomon are taken from the garments of

the Byzantine Emperors: but that the miniaturist trans-

ferred his thought from the Gospel narrative to contemporary

- 67 -   Page XVII

reality, does not appear from the design. The probability
of this supposition is particularly weakened by the fact
that in the other Gospels written later than the X century and at a time when not two Emperors were reigning,
but one, the same kings David and Solomon appear and in
the same Imperial garments. So only the character of the
calligraphy and the style of the miniatures are left as
indications of the antiquity of the manuscript. There is
a miniature picture of this Evangelist before the Gospel
of Mark; and then the beginning of the text until the
words   is separated as a subject
for the illustrations. Here are represented (sheet 64
and on the reverse): the prophet Isaiah and John the
Baptist with the open scrolls (Mark I, 2-4); lower -
John baptising the people;⁽⁵ the meeting of John the   Page XVIII
Baptist with Jesus Christ and the sermon of John the
Baptist (sheet 65). Before the Gospel of Luke is the
picture of this Evangelist, with short and thick hair
and a hardly noticeable beard (sheet 101 on the reverse)
and also a picture of the reigning prince Theophilus
in Byzantine garments decorated with tablion (sheet 102);
to the same place belong the episodes from the history
of Zacharias: he is standing with Elisabeth swinging

a censer before the sacrificial altar and an angel is
appearing before him; Zacharias, stupefied, is coming
from the temple to the astonished throng of people
(sheet 102-103). Before the Gospel of John: Evangelist
John (sheet 157 on the reverse). The Holy Trinity [1]

----
[1] According to N.P. Kondakov (p. 250) Glory of Our Lord
----

the sermon of John (sheet 158), the sermon of Jesus
Christ to the people (John I, 10-11), who are running
away from him, and a sermon before another group of
people who listen to him attentively with heads bowed
(p. 12): these are the future apostles with Peter at
their head. In this codex the attempt at bringing together miniatures and the text of the Gospel is not
brought to an end. The miniaturist does not go into the
depth of content of the Gospels and does not try to
depict the main features of their difference which would
be important for the completeness of the illustrations
of Gospel history. He takes only the first verses of
the Gospels and uses them as the first sign of the
Gospels.   2) The Gospel of Athos-Iversky Monastery,
XII - XIII centuries (No. and in 4) illuminated by the
miniatures on a golden background in size of half a

page.(2   In spite of the comparatively late appearance of

----

2) The photographic reproductions of them in the album of
   Sevastianov (Moscow Public Museum) are not satisfactory.

----

this codex, its miniatures are still reminiscent of the

brilliant epoch, full of life and energy, of Byzantine

art. Though resembling closely in style and coloring the

miniatures of the Gelat Gospel of the XII century,(3

----

3) See below.

----

they surpass them in fineness of workmanship, nearness to

nature, variety and beauty of the types. In the miniature

of the Nativity of Christ (sheet 8) the small figures have

extraordinarily fine and regular countenances: the ex-

cellent figures in the picture of the raising from the

dead of Lazarus (sheet 415) have life and individuality

and are beautifully draped in a variety of garments. The

annunciating angel has sufficiently natural movement

(sheet 222); even the naked body of Jesus Christ, which

ordinarily is a stumbling block for the Byzantine artists

is executed satisfactorily. The compositions are in

general successful; sometimes the miniaturist is trying

to introduce in the usual themes a sparkle of vividness

(compare the picture of the possessed gesticulating with

his arms, with disheveled hair (sheet 156); also the

representation of the son of the courtier in a death

agony (sheet 177 on the reverse). The coloring has

variety, and although the predominating colors are blue,

red andpurple, the shades are pleasant. In the Gospel

of Matthew we have eight pictures: the Nativity of Christ,

the healing of two possessed in the country of the

Gergesenes, the healing of the woman with the issue of

blood, the miracle of the loaves and fishes, the parable

of the guest invited to the feast, the Last Supper, the

descent of the body of Jesus Christ from the cross, and

the appearance of Jesus Christ to the women after the

resurrection. In the Gospel of Mark are eight; the

Evangelist Mark himself, the baptism of Jesus Christ,

the healing of the mother-in-law of Simon,/the leper,
                                        of

of the possessed and of the son of the courtier, and the

crucifixion of Jesus Christ in two aspects. In the

Gospel of Luke are seven: the Evangelist Luke, the

Annunciation, the Presentation, the Transfiguration,

the healing of those suffering from the dropsy, the

parable of the rich man and Lazarus, and the widow's

mite; in the Gospel of John are twelve: the Evangelist

John twice; the wedding in Cana, the discourse with the

Samaritan woman, the healing of the paralytic and the

blind, the raising from the dead of Lazarus, the entry

of Jesus Christ into Jerusalem, the washing of feet,
and three additional miniatures. John Chrysostom in
phelonion with a scroll is standing before Jesus Christ.
The Mother of God with a scroll is leading young
Chrysostom to Jesus Christ, and two episodes from the
story of the appearance of God to Abraham in the dis-
guise of three pilgrims. 3) The illuminated Gospel of
the Athos-Vatopedy Monastery (No. 101-735) is near in
time to the above-mentioned Gospel but considerably
lower in its artistic quality: the colors are muddy
and crude, the poses of the figures are monotonous and
rigid, the types are not consistent; the faces are
copper-red and almost all enlivened with the same un-
natural blush; instead of eyes are black spots with
white dashes. The compositions are copied from examples
themselves not bad, the merits of which are noticeable
in the miniature of the Nativity of Christ, well composed (sheet 15). The trend toward naturalism and live-
liness is one of the peculiarities of the miniaturist,
but he lacks schooling and taste. In the picture of the
crucifixion the Mother of God lifts her head unnaturally
and wipes away the tears (sheet 18). The Savior on the
cross, the Apostle John in the same picture of the crucifixion, the angels in the picture of the Ascension
(sheet 19), the Mother of God (sheet 201 on the reverse)

are unnaturally bent; the holy Marys are sitting near

the sarcophagus of Our Lord and gesticulating; unbound

hair appears from their headdress. The miniaturist pro-

fusely illustrates the Gospel of Matthew (11 miniatures)

but he leaves the Gospels of Mark and John without minia-

tures (only the pictures of the Evangelists), and in the

Gospel of Luke he inserted the Annunciation. The chron-

ological order of the text is broken in the miniatures:

the descent of the body of Jesus Christ precedes the cruci-

fixion. In the Gospel of Matthew there are inserted pic-

tures among others, of the purification, the Ascension,

and the descent of the Holy Ghost on the apostles, about

which there is nothing in the text of the Evangelist.

The miniatures have captions above indicating the con-

tent (for instance

and captions below are of an edifying character (for in- Page XIX

stance,

In this Gospel we find among other things separate pic-

tures of the symbols of the Evangelists, prohibited by

the Russian church and also the tetramorph, that is, a

group of four symbols of the evangelists with a sign of

liturgic origin: an eagle =
                                                    (1
an ox =   a lion=   a man =
----
1) Compare the explanation of the patriarch of Constantinople
   Hermogen: writing of the Fathers and teachers of the church

4) Nicodemus Gospel of the XIII century in the ecclesiastico-
archaeological museum at Kiev theological academy. The
number of miniatures is not considerable: two in the
Gospel of Matthew, two in Mark, three in Luke, and ten
in John. At the beginning of the first three Gospels the
miniaturist places the pictures of the Evangelists, and
besides that, in the Gospel of Luke the Annunciation of
the Mother of God. At the end of the Gospel of Matthew -
the apparition of the resurrected Savior to the Holy
Marys (sheet 92), at the end of the Gospel of Mark -
the ascension of Our Lord (sheet 151), at the end of
the Gospel of Luke - the Apparition of the angel to the
holy women after the resurrection of Jesus Christ, and
the Apostle Peter beside the sarcophagus of Jesus Christ
(sheet 246). In the Gospel of John are: the meeting of
John the Baptist with the Savior, the healing of the
blind and events beginning from the raising from the
dead of Lazarus until the convincing of the Apostle
Thomas.[2 In the beginning of the Gospel there are two

----

2) The comparison of the miniatures of this Gospel with
the miniatures of the Gelat Gospel and with the fres-
coes in St.Sophia's Cathedral in Kiev are to be found
in the paper of Prof. N.I.Petrov: the Proceedings of
the V Archaeological Congress in Tiflis, pp. 170-179;
also phototypic pictures of two miniatures.

extra miniatures: Emmanual in an almond-shaped nimbus
with four symbols of the Evangelists and the Mother of
God on the throne with the baby Jesus. From the point
of view of iconographic composition the miniatures of
this codex stand very near to the Gelat Gospel, as it is
proved by N.I. Petrov,[3] but in their artistic style they
----
[3] Ibid.
----
are lower than the latter: this Gospel is reminiscent
of the decadent epoch of Byzantine art in its long
lean figures on thin legs (John the Baptist on sheet 254 ;
the Apostle Peter in the picture of the washing of the
feet on sheet 298), in the tendency to increase the significance of the person portrayed through the increase
of the dimentions (Jesus Christ in the healing of the
blind on sheet 284). Two groups of apostles in the picture of the Ascension are well composed, the countenance
of Emmanuel with the regular and attractive features is
beautifully done, which is an echo of a good school,
this being revealed also in the predominance of the light
coloring. 5) The Gospel of the Library of Athens Uni-
versity of the XII century (No.6). In this codex one
notices the tendency of the artist to illustrate the last
events of the terrestrial life of Jesus Christ. Although
this attempt is not followed with strict consequence,

nevertheless it can have its importance. It is connected
with those illuminations of the Passion that later on
were so widespread in Western Europe and Russia. What
connection such attempts have with the latest codices
of the Passion is impossible to decide at present, on
account of the lack of Byzantine monuments. The total
number of the miniatures in the Athens Gospel reached
21, and three Evangelists: Mark, Luke and John. The
miniatures are made by different hands; from the beginning to sheet 194 inclusive they are quite large
(the sixth part of a half sheet); here we find the
arrest of Jesus Christ in the Garden of Gethsemane,
the weeping holy women, the Judeans before Pilate, the
healing of the blind, Jesus Christ on the way to Pilate,
the carrying of the cross, Joseph of Arimathea before
Pilate, the healing of the lepers and of the halt.
Then from sheet 247 there are small miniatures reminding
one of the miniatures of the Gelat Gospel: the parable
of the wicked slave, the publican and the Pharisee, the
entry into Jerusalem, the Last Supper, Jesus Christ before Pilate and the meeting of Jesus Christ with John:
beginning at sheet 297 the miniatures are again larger,
as in the beginning: the discourse with the Samaritan
woman, the raising from the dead of Lazarus, the Last

Supper, the crucifixion of Jesus Christ and the convincing

of Thomas. These latter are of a better quality than in the

Gelat Gospel: the brush is lively and the colors are lighter

than in the preceding group, the countenances are finely

finished, the postures of the figures are correct, the com-

position of the subjects is worked out very well (compare

the raising from the dead of Lazarus with the discourse with

the Samaritan woman); each miniature is provided with a cap-

tion. 6) The Greek Gospel of the Imperial Public Library in

St. Petersburg of the XII - XIII centuries (No.1 105)[4]

----

[4] Compare Archimandrite Amphiloch. As to miniatures in the
Greek manuscript in the Imperial Public Library, p. 332
and following.

The miniaturist illustrates the text sufficiently in detail

and places in the Gospel of Matthew 16 miniatures, in the

Gospel of Mark 11, in the Gospel of Luke 24, and in the Gos-

pel of John 13; besides that, in the beginning of the Gospels

there are the pictures of the Evangelists (John is placed

wrongly) and the bust picture of Emmanuel, as the source and

the main subject of all Gospel narratives. Evidently the

miniaturist copied from the complete codex, curtailing the

number of its miniatures and the details of the compositions

and choosing only some miniatures according to his own

judgment; in that way it happened that on account of/in-

sufficient competence of the copyist, some important events

are left without illustrations and vice versa, he illuminated Page XX

events of secondary importance, having significance only in

being introductory to the others (compare sheet 165 on the

reverse: Jesus Christ is sending his disciples for the she
ass, sheet 169- the entry into the prepared chamber); some
subjects are repeated. In the Gospel of Matthew are pictured: the adoration by the Magi (sheet 12 on the reverse),
the slaughter of the first born of Bethlehem (sheet 13),
the baptism of Jesus Christ (sheet 15), the healing of the
lepers (sheet 22), of the mother-in-law of Simon (sheet 23),
of the two lunatics (sheet 24), the transfiguration (sheet 40),
the entry into Jerusalem (sheet 47), the Last Supper (sheet 60),
the praying in the Garden of Gethsemane (sheet 61), the
betrayal by Judas (sheet 62), the crucifixion (sheet 65),
the resurrection and the descent into hell (sheet 67), the
appearance of the resurrected Savior to the Holy Women
(sheet 68); in the Gospel of Mark: the healing of the half
(sheet 72) of the one with the withered arm (sheet 74), of
the woman with the issue of blood (sheet 79), the transfiguration (sheet 87), the dry fig tree (sheet 93), the prophecy
of the destruction of Jerusalem (sheet 97), the women anoint-
ing the feet of Jesus Christ (sheet 99), Jesus Christ before
Pilate (sheet 103) and the Ascension (sheet 106 on the reverse); in the Gospel of Luke there are: the Annunciation
(sheet 110), the purification (sheet 114), the miracle of
the draught of fishes (sheet 127), the healing of the lunatic
(sheet 132), Jesus Christ blessing the apostles (sheet 129),

the feeding of the multitude (sheet 130), the transfiguration (sheet 131), the healing of the lunatic (sheet 132),
of the sufferer from dropsy (sheet 144), and of ten lepers
(sheet 150), the publican and the Pharisee (sheet 162),
on the tree (sheet 164), Jesus Christ sending
his disciples for an ass (sheet 165 on the reverse), the
entry into Jerusalem (sheet 166), the widow)s mite (sheet
169 on the reverse), the entry into the chamber and the
prayer in the Garden of Gethsemane (sheet 173), the bear-
ing of the cross (sheet 176), the crucifixion (sheet 176),
the laying into the tomb, (sheet 178), Peter beside the
sarcophagus of Jesus Christ (sheet 179), the benediction
of the apostles (sheet 181). In the Gospel of John
there are: the wedding in Cana (sheet 185), the discourse
with the Samaritan woman (sheet 189), the healing of
the halt (sheet 192), the feeding of the multitude (sheet
192 on the reverse), the walking on the water of Jesus
Christ (sheet 193 on the reverse), the betrayal by Judas
(sheet 214), the crucifixion (sheet 217), the laying into
the tomb (sheet 218), the epiphany of Jesus Christ after
the resurrection to the apostle Thomas (sheet 220),and
on the Lake of Tiberias (sheet 221), the breaking of bread
on the seashore (sheet 222). 7) The Gospel of the Paris
National Library - of the XIII century (No. 54). It is

written in two columns: in one the text is Greek and in

the other it is Latin and not complete.[1] It is reasonable

----

[1] On pages 141 to 279 there is no Latin text.

----

to suppose that it was predetermined for the Western

Christians of Southern Italy and Sicily who were using the

Eastern ritual and the Greek language. The original in-

tention to decorate the entire text with the miniatures was

left unfulfilled: some miniatures are outlined only in

contour; for the others empty spaces were left. This

PICTURE

Caption - 4. The Baptism of Jesus Christ. From Gospel No.54.

circumstance helps to explain the method which the minia-

turist used in his work, as Bordier has already mentioned.[2]

----

[2] Descript. p. 228.

First he would draw in ink the main outlines of the en-

tire picture and in this way he would lay the basic idea

of it; then he would put a golden background made from

little sheets of gold, probably with the help of white of

egg and starch; then with a fine brush he would outline

with brownish color the main parts of the design, to de-
fine more exactly and fix the idea. Finally he would pass
on to the finishing of details. The mechanical attitude
of the miniaturist toward the illuminating is clearly
seen in the method of coloring of miniatures. He would
take one color and would paint with it simultaneously all
parts of the pictures, according to his plan, that required that particular color, so that the picture, after
this operation, presented a series, for instance, only
of red spots. (Sheet 201). Then he would pass on to
the other colors. Bordier finds these miniatures valuable
and beautiful; this praise is exaggerated: the coloring
of the miniature is reminiscent of the Athos-Vatopedys
codex: iconographical types are not strictly executed;
the type of the Savior with chestnut hair and undivided
beard is satisfactory, but the characteristic type of
the apostle Peter is garbled, so that it is unrecognizable.
The unusual freedom of the contours in the pictures of
the Evangelists gives us reason to compare them with the
Western codices of the XIII century. The free attitude
toward iconographic tradition is noticeable also in the
exchange of the landscape for the buildings in the picture
of the arrest of the Savior in the Garden of Gethsemane
(sheet 38 on the reverse), and in the figure of the

personification of the sea - a woman sitting in a small

boat. The number of miniatures in the Gospel of Matthew   Page XXI

is 13, of Mark - 6, of Luke - 11, of John - 2.[1

----

1) The description by Bordier pp. 228-231; compare the
cited works of Kondakov (p. 245), where the parable
of the guest invited to the feast is expounded as a
parable of the tares, and the miniature itself is
not described entirely exactly.

----

8) The Greek Gospel of the Imperial Public Library in

St. Petersburg (No. 118).[2 The clear indication of the
----

2) Compare the cited works of the Archimandrite Amphilachy
p. 54 and following.

----

writing of this manuscript is to be found in the picture

of a man on his knees in the garments of the Byzantine

Emperor with the sign

on sheet 383. On sheet 3 in the middle of the double-

headed eagle we find a monogram of the Palaeologi, and

on sheet 22 is Michael Palaeologus in a red hat with

the caption

So the codex is from the reign of Michael Palaeologus

about the year 1450. The miniatures of this Gospel pre-

sent mainly the festivals of the Orthodox church. This

choice is explained by the fact that toward the XV cen-

tury, with the multiplication of the festivals of this

church, the significance of Gospel events in honor of
which special festivals were established increased in
the eyes of artists, Although at the beginning of the
Gospel on three sheets preceding the index of the Gospel
readings there are to be found pictures of the parable
of the sower (sheet 1), the discourse with the Samaritan
woman (sheet 2), the stilling of the tempest (sheet 3
on the reverse), and a few miniatures not belonging to
the text of the Gospel, including the Emperor Constantine
and Helena [3] with a cross between them, the miniatures in
----
[3] According to Muralt Irine (Catal.)
----
the Gospel of Matthew begin with the Annunciation (sheet
21), which shows the free attitude of the miniaturist
toward the text. After it the Nativity of Christ (sheet
21 on the reverse), the purification (sheet 22 on the
reverse), the baptism of Jesus Christ (sheet 23), the
transfiguration (sheet 122 on the reverse), the raising
from the dead of Lazarus (sheet 124 on the reverse) [4]
----
[4] This miniature should be in the Gospel of John.
----
and the entry into Jerusalem (sheet 125); in the Gospel
of Mark the crucifixion (sheet 190 on the reverse), the

descent into hell (sheet 193 on the reverse), and the
Ascension of Jesus Christ to heaven (sheet 194); in the
Gospel of Luke the descent of the Holy Ghost on the apostles
(sheet 300), the assumption of the Mother of God (sheet
301); in the Gospel of John the Last Supper (sheet 384),
and the washing of the feet (sheet 384 on the reverse).
Obviously the miniaturist chooses from the Gospel very
little, arranges the events in their chronological order,
and brings here the pictures which do not refer directly
to the Gospel; such is the assumption of the Mother of
                                           the
God which, together with the pictures of/Palaeologi,
give us reason to suppose that this manuscript had its
origin either in Constantinople or Athos. The opinion of
Muralt that the greatest part of the miniatures (except
the Evangelists and Demetrius Palaeologus) were made in
Italy has only one correct part - that the influence of
the Western school is reflected on them, namely in the
landscape scenes, the aerial perspective and some iconographic details; but the general character of the compositions and the Greek captions (   )
give us rather reason to believe that the miniatures were
executed by a Greek who had acquaintance with the Western
painting.

III. In the series of the complete illuminated

Greek Gospels the first place must be given 1) to the

Gospel of the Paris National Library, of the XI century

(No. 74). By reason of the completeness of the icono-

graphical material, preservation, the freshness of the

colors and its icon-painting beauty, this is the best of

all Byzantine illuminated Gospels that has reached us.

These merits compensate partly for the noticeable lack

of inventiveness, anatomical mistakes and incorrectness

in the postures of some figures.[5]

----

[5] Compare Waagen Kunstwerke u. Künstler in Parks
S. 226-227. N.P.Kondakov History of Byzantine
Art pp. 237-240. Bordier Desci. 113-36. Some pic-
tures in Labarte (Hist. des arts). Pogo de Fleury
(L'Evangile) and Grimoir Guide de l'art chr.

Its miniatures embrace not only the most important

events of the Gospel but also the details of the dis-

courses, sermons, parables and similes. Step by step the

artist follows the text of the Gospel, transferring

this text sometimes to the miniature in the smallest de-

tail. Here we see, for instance how the Savior is anoint-

ing the eyes of the blind man with clay, how the guide

is leading this blind man to the pool of Siloam, the

blind man coming to the pool and returning healed, telling

the people about his being healed, the parents of the blind

man being asked to explain, here again the healed man

himself coming, the people chasing him away and he
kneeling before Jesus Christ (sheets 186 - 187 on the
reverse). All these details of the Gospel narrative
expressed in separate miniatures.[6] The character of

----

[6] The figures are about 3 centimeters high.

----

the sermons and parables with their many shadings, particularly complicated the work of the miniaturist: we
see here, for instance, how the sower is casting seeds,
how these seeds have germinated - some on stony ground,
some among thorns, some are being picked up by birds,
some have ripened on fertile ground; the reaper mowing
the stout ears (70). A separate picture of the Savior
on the throne, teaching his apostles, indicates that
all these details do not express an historical fact,
but only a supplementary narrative. With as many details are presented the parable of the prodigal son
(sheet 143), the healing of the lunatic (sheet 83) and
the others. The total number of the miniatures in the
Gospel of Matthew reaches 99, in the Gospel of Mark -   Page XXII
67, in the Gospel of Luke - 97, and in the Gospel of
John - 86.[1] Displaying such servility toward the text

----

[1] Bordier, dividing some miniatures in two parts, sug-
    gests a different enumeration: 110, 67, 103 and 95.
    Bordier p. 136.

----

and putting literalism among the basic requirements of
Gospel iconography, the artist necessarily would have to
permit repetition of themes, because he would find in
the different Evangelists narratives of the same events.
Such repetitions are not rare, but the miniatures repeated are not entirely identical and allow shadings
according to the peculiarities in the narratives of the
different Evangelists. There are not here even two identical miniatures. But revealing in this case a sensible
and not mechanical attitude, the miniaturist discloses
in many instances that he copied from existing originals
and has no understanding of the significance of the ancient
iconographical details; for instance, the meaning of the
nimbus. We have reason to think that in the most ancient
illuminated Gospels, the apostles in the pictures of
the events of the terrestrial life of Jesus Christ were
represented without the nimbus, and only in the events
of their lives beginning from the descent of the Holy
Ghost was the ninbus used, as an external sign of blessed
gifts and authority. As an example we point out the
Gospels of the Rossano codex, the Syrian Gospel, the Gospel
of Rabula, and the Trapesund Gospel of the Imperial Public Library in St.Petersburg (No. 21). While the

miniaturist of the codex under consideration uses the
nimbus without any specific order: the same persons in
very similar situations are represented here sometimes
with the nimbus and sometimes without; in the same group
of the apostles some of them have the nimbus and some
have not (sheet 124 on the reverse); in the picture of
the descent from the cross the companion of the Mother
of God has a nimbus and the favorite disciple of Christ
has none (sheet 208 on the reverse); in one of the pictures of the crucifixion the same companion has no nimbus.
This inconsistency gives us an opportunity to see that
the ancient point of view on the significance of the
nimbus had no particular importance in the eyes of our
miniaturist, although he preserved an echo of this tradition in the nimbus of Herod (sheet 4). The traditions
of classic antiquity appear in weak traces in the miniatures: the miniaturist represents with sufficient realism
a building with an antique portico in the picture of the
resurrection of the daughter of Archon (sheet 17 on
the reverse), an antique pool in the picture of the
annunciation of the holy Mother of God (sheet 105 on
the reverse, compare with sheet 176). He introduces in
the miniature the personifications of the wind and the
River Jordan, changing the latter into the form of a boy

(sheet 64 on the reverse). This shows that the personification of the Jordan was not clear for our copyist:
evidently some details of the complicated picture of the
crucifixion are also not clear (sheet 59). Side by side
with the antique elements, there are some details in the
miniatures borrowed from the Byzantine mode of life.
For instance, the garments, and the mourners in the form
of women with unbound hair in the picture of the resurrection of the son of the widow of Nain (sheet 121). But
in general the miniaturist follows the antique traditions
of Byzantine iconography and firmly remembers that the
foundation of his subject must be the Gospel text. It
is impossible to deny that he knew some of the traditions,
the origin of which is vague, and which are attributed
to apocryphic sources, but it is difficult to agree with
a well-known specialist of the history of the Byzantine
miniature, that the miniaturist, representing in detail
the history of the annunciation and Nativity of Christ
were using all the known apocryphies without discrimination.[2]
----
[2] N. P. Kondakov, History of Byzantine Art, p. 238.
By the way, we wish to correct an error which gives
the author an opportunity to reprove the miniaturist
for a display of bad taste in icon painting: this is
the supposed representation of Jesus Christ with a
broom, searching for a lost drachma (Ibid. pp. 139 and
239). This picture is to be found on the reverse of
sheet 142; however it is not Jesus Christ with the broom,
but the woman who lost the drachma, which is in accordance with the Gospel text (Luke XV, 8-9).

The annunciation is represented here only at one moment
"beside the fountain", and there is no detailed development of the themes offered by the apocryphies. The Nativity of Christ is represented in the Gospels of Matthew
and Luke in more detail, but here also we do not find
indiscriminate use of the apocryphies. The miniaturist is
copying from existing originals and repeats those forms
which long ago were accepted in artistic practice. The
annunciation beside a fountain is known in the monuments
of the V and VI centuries; the details of the Nativity
of Christ repeated by the miniaturist are to be found
in antiquo-Christian sculpture. In the other miniatures
he has also elements that are connected with the apocryphic
traditions; but these elements, considering the
entire aggregation of the miniatures, do not occupy a
noticeable place and do not penetrate into the depth of
illustrations. The whole would not suffer very much if
we were to throw aside these traditional elements. From
this point of view this codex could not stand comparison
with the known homilies of Jacob, the mosaics of the
Constantinople Cathedral of Our Savior or with the sculpture of the Ravennate pulpit of Maximilian. The main
iconographic forms of miniatures of this codex find their
explanation in the Gospel text.

2) An example of the same version is represented
by the Slavonic Gospel of the Pecrovsky Edinoverchesky
Church in the city of Elisavetgrad. The spelling of the
codex is Bulgarian; the antiquity is not earlier than
the XIV century, because in the synoxar appended to the   Page XXIII
Gospel there are to be found the names of the Serbian
saints - Simeon and Bishop Savva (XIII century).[1   It
----
1) Bishop Sergius Agiologia II, pp. 11, 38, 53.
----
is written in excellent script of the XIV-XV centuries on
perchment in folio. The general character of the miniatures is the same as those in the Paris Gospel No. 74:
the same completeness of iconographic content, the same
compositions, partly the same mistakes and misunderstand-
ings. We present for comparison a few pictures, relating
to the last days of John the Precursor, taken from both
codices. The difference between the Elisavetgrad Gospel
and the Paris is in details. In the beginning of the Gospel of Matthew, in a vignette in five medallions around
the Evangelist Matthew there are represented Abraham,
Isaac, Jacob, with scrolls in their hands and two cheru-
bims; in the Paris Gospel, instead of Abraham, there is
represented the Ancient of Days - the Savior in the image
of an old man in a tunic and himation with scroll and a
sign (   ). A close resemblance of

this picture of Abraham with the pictures of Isaac and

Jacob in the Elisavetgrad Gospel gives us reason to

think that the miniaturist of this Gospel really in-

tended Abraham here, but not the Ancient of Days; prob-

ably the figure of the original from which he had copied

had not had a caption, which is to be found in the Paris

codex; the fact that the miniaturist of the Paris codex

interpreted the significance of this figure correctly,

taking it for the Savior but not Abraham, is proved by

the repetition of the pictures of the same Savior in

different aspects on the corresponding places of the

vignettes of all the other Evangelists, as in the Paris

and the Elisavetgrad codices. In the same vignette

PICTURE

Caption.5. Paris Gospel No. 74

- - - - -

PICTURE

Caption.6.Elisavetgrad Gospel

- - - - -

below, Evangelist Matthew is standing before an un-

identified person dressed in the garments of a Byzantine

Emperor: but in the Paris codex the picture of an Em-

peror is replaced by the picture of an abbot and it is

placed at the end of the Gospel of Matthew. This latter

difference caused us to think that the Paris Gospel

had a monastic origin and destination, while the

Elisavetgrad one, or at least the original of it, was

intended as a gift to a sovereign. The whole content

of the miniatures in both Gospels is identical. In

the Elisavetgrad Gospel there are missing/few miniatures

which have second rate significance, and namely, in the

Gospel of Matthew, Jesus Christ and the apostles on

the way to Mount Eleon (Paris Gospel, sheet 53 on the

reverse) and the bringing of Jesus Christ to the judgment

of the Chief Priest (Paris Gospel, sheet 56 on the re-

verse), the third picture of the crucifixion (Paris

Gospel, sheet 59 on the reverse); in the Gospel of

Mark there are missing the second picture of the prayer

of Jesus Christ in the Garden of Gethsemane,/the descent

of Jesus Christ into hell; in the Gospel of Luke there

are missing three pictures referring to Luke IV, 20,

and the following; IX, 48 and 52-53; the resurrection

of the son of the widow of Nain (Luke VII, 11 and the

following) the discourses of Jesus Christ with a lawyer

(X, 25), the accusing of the Pharisees (XI, 42), ref-

erence to the birds which do not sow and do not harvest

(XII, 24), to the didrachma (XV, 8-9); in the Gospel of

John there is missing the second picture of the preaching

of Jesus Christ about the daily bread (Chapter VI). All

these omissions do no damage at all to the whole: almost

all the omitted miniatures belong to the type of com- Page XXIV

positions which are repeated in the codex many times, and

therefore do not represent any particular interest. The

rest of the miniatures in both codices are entirely in

conformity. The differences in detail of the pictures

are insignificant; for instance, in the picture of the

Nativity of Christ (in the Gospel of Matthew) the minia-

turist of the Elisavetgrad Gospel omits the cave, the

beams emanating from the hand of the angel, the figure of

the little goat; in the picture of the Baptism he omits

the branch in the beak of the pigeon - the Holy Ghost,

the star, the hand of God the Father and the cross in

the water; the picture of the ascension of Our Lord is

supplemented by two angels; the Mother of God is placed

between two groups of apostles, and the halo of the

Savior has the form of a many-colored sphere.

www.ingramcontent.com/pod-product-compliance
Lightning Source LLC
Chambersburg PA
CBHW031105020726
47495CB00007B/2050